This book belongs to

Sofiia

make believe ideas

The Gingerbread Man

Key sound ay spellings: a, ai, ay, ey
Secondary sounds: ea, er, ite

Written by Nick Page
Illustrated by Clare Fennell

Reading with phonics

How to use this book

The **Reading with phonics** series helps you to have fun with your child and to support their learning of phonics and reading. It is aimed at children who have learned the letter sounds and are building confidence in their reading.

Each title in the series focuses on a different key sound. The entertaining retelling of the story repeats this sound frequently, and the different spellings for the sound are highlighted in red type. The first activity at the back of the book provides practice in reading and using words that contain this sound. The key sound for **The Gingerbread Man** is ay.

Start by reading the story to your child, asking them to join in with the refrain in bold. Next, encourage them to read the story with you. Give them a hand to decode tricky words.

Now look at the activity pages at the back of the book. These are intended for you and your child to enjoy together. Most are not activities to complete in pencil or pen, but by reading and talking or pointing.

The **Key sound** pages focus on one sound, and on the various different groups of letters that produce that sound. Encourage your child to read the different letter groups and complete the activity, so they become more aware of the variety of spellings there are for the same sound.

The **Letters together** pages look at three pairs or groups of letters and at the sounds they make as they work together. Help your child to read the words and trace the route on the word maps.

Rhyme is used a lot in these retellings. Whatever stage your child has reached in their learning of phonics, it is always good practice for them to listen carefully for sounds and find words that rhyme. The pages on **Rhyming words** take six words from the story and ask children to read and find other words that rhyme with them.

The **Sight words** pages focus on a number of sight words that occur regularly but can nonetheless be challenging. Many of these words are not sounded out following the rules of phonics and the easiest thing is for children to learn them by sight, so that they do not worry about decoding them. These pages encourage children to retell the story, practicing sight words as they do so.

The **Picture dictionary** page asks children to focus closely on nine words from the story. Encourage children to look carefully at each word, cover it with their hand, write it on a separate piece of paper, and finally, check it!

Do not complete all the activities at once – doing one each time you read will ensure that your child continues to enjoy the stories and the time you are spending together. **Have fun!**

There once was a crazy, old baker
and a crazy, old baker's wife,
and one day they made a gingerbread man,
who amazingly came to life!

The name that they gave him
was Gingerbread Fred
and they said, "Don't you wander away!
You are not a real boy, you're a pastry,
like the ones they serve in the café!"

But before you could say,

"CAKES AND BAGELS,"

Fred wouldn't obey – he ran off to play!

And Gingerbread Fred said . . .

"Run, run, run, as fast as you can,
you can't catch me,
I'm the gingerbread man!"

He made his way into a playground,
where a cat lay asleep by the gate.
"Oh, meow," said the cat.
"Here comes breakfast,
I wondered how long I should wait."

Meow!

But before you could say,

"CAKES AND BAGELS,"

Fred didn't delay,

but went on his way!

And Gingerbread Fred said . . .

10

"Run, run, run, as fast as you can,
you can't catch me,
I'm the gingerbread man!"

Next, Gingerbread Fred reached a farmyard,
where a dog lay asleep in the hay.
"Oh, BOW-WOW!" said the dog.
"Must be lunchtime!
It's a gingerbread-cake
takeaway!

Bow-wow!

But before you could say,
"CAKES AND BAGELS,"
Fred wouldn't remain,
but raced down the lane!

And Gingerbread Fred said . . .

"Run, run, run, as fast as you can,
you can't catch me,
I'm the gingerbread man!"

Then Gingerbread Fred reached the lakeside,

"Good day," said a fox by the bay.

"Need my aid?" said the fox. "I can take you.

You can ride on my back, just one way."

And before you could say,

"CAKES AND BAGELS,"

Fred was persuaded, and in the fox waded.

And Gingerbread Fred said . . .

"Run, run, run, as fast as you can,
you can't catch me,
I'm the gingerbread man!"

17

The fox said, "May I make a suggestion?"
as they made their way over the bay.
"If you stay on my nose, you'll be drier,
and avoid all this splashing and spray."

Quite soon, they were over the water,
and Fred said, "Good day!
Thanks again!"

"Not so fast," said the fox,
"I've a brainwave,
would you like to fly,
just like a plane?"

21

And before you could say,
"CAKES AND BAGELS,"
with a cry of "wa-hey,"
Fred flew away!

And Gingerbread Fred said . . .

"Run, run, run, as fast as you can,
you can't catch me, I'm the . . ."

CRUNCH! SCRUNCH! MUNCH!

Fox ate him for lunch.

And Gingerbread Fred said . . .

Nothing. (Ever again.)

CRUNCH!

SCRUNCH!

MUNCH!

Key sound

There are several different groups of letters that make the ay sound. Practice them by helping Gingerbread Fred make some sentences. Use each word in the bagels in a different sentence.

they
convey
obey
survey
prey

baker made
ate lake came
lane persuade
race plane gave
take gate wave make bagel cake made

remain rain main train wait aid plain brain

say play stay day lay spray delay bay hay playground away replay

Letters together

Look at these groups of letters and say the sounds they make.

ea   **er**   **ite**

Follow the words that contain ea to help the baker find his bread.

ea

right

chips   tread

child   head

from   dead

bread   chair

right

Follow the words that contain er to help the fox cross the river.

lots

er

other

later

dinner

water

fern

planner

cake

river · · · · runner

Follow the words that contain ite to help the fox bite the biscuit.

suddenly

mite

ite

kite · · · · white

site

quite · · write

bite

27

Rhyming words

Read the words in the flowers and point to other words that rhyme with them.

café	**cake**	bake
pastry		shake

gate	**dog**	run
frog		log

hat	**cat**	plane
bat		fly

life	knife
lunch	back

wife

main	baker
bay	grain

brain

lakeside	rose
hose	flew

nose

Now choose a word and make up a rhyming chant!

The baker **bakes** **cakes** and **makes** **milkshakes**.

Sight words

Many common words can be difficult to sound out. Practice them by reading these sentences about the story. Now make more sentences using other sight words from around the border.

The fox ate Fred **for** lunch.

The cat and dog **couldn't** catch Fred.

The baker said to Fred, "**Don't** you wander away!"

The baker **made** a gingerbread man.

The **cat** chased Gingerbread Fred.

The gingerbread man **ran** from the baker.

something · animals · looked · got · it

· couldn't · town · a · sat · run · made · are · ran · we